· HARRIET'S ·
HALLOWEEN CANDY

· HARRIET'S ·
HALLOWEEN CANDY

Nancy Carlson

PUFFIN BOOKS

for my sister, Tuden, because she taught me to draw,
and for my brother, David, because he withstood
so much teasing and still grew up to be a nice guy!

PUFFIN BOOKS
Published by the Penguin Group
Viking Penguin Inc., 40 West 23rd Street, New York, New York 10010, U.S.A.
Penguin Books Ltd, 27 Wrights Lane, London W8 5TZ England
Penguin Books Australia Ltd, Ringwood, Victoria, Australia
Penguin Books Canada Ltd, 2801 John Street, Markham, Ontario, Canada L3R 1B4
Penguin Books (N.Z.) Ltd, 182-190 Wairau Road, Auckland 10, New Zealand

Penguin Books Ltd, Registered Offices: Harmondsworth, Middlesex, England

First published in the United States of America by Carolrhoda Books, Inc., Minneapolis, 1982
Published in Picture Puffins 1984
5   7   9   10   8   6
Copyright © CAROLRHODA BOOKS, INC., 1982
All rights reserved

Library of Congress Cataloging in Publication Data
Carlson, Nancy L.
Harriet's Halloween candy.
Summary: Harriet learns the hard way that sharing her
Halloween candy makes her feel much better than eating it
all herself.
[1. Halloween—Fiction. 2. Sharing—Fiction. 3. Candy
—Fiction. 4. Dogs—Fiction] I. Title.
PZ7.C21665Har 1984 [E] 83-43282
ISBN 0-14-050465-6

Printed in the United States of America
by Lake Book/Cuneo, Inc., Melrose Park, Illinois

Harriet really got a lot of candy on Halloween.

When she got home, she laid it all out carefully on the floor. Then she organized it. First by color. Then by size. And finally by favorites.

Harriet's little brother Walter watched. He was too little to go trick-or-treating.

"Harriet, you be sure you share your candy
with Walt," said Harriet's mother.

"No!" said Harriet. "It's all mine."

But Harriet felt a little guilty.

"Oh, all right," she said. She reached into her
bag and pulled out a teensy-weensy piece of
coconut candy.

Harriet didn't like coconut anyway.

Before Harriet went to bed, she packed her candy in a big box.

Then she hid the box in her closet.

The next morning she got up early to eat some of her candy.

After she finished three caramel-chocolate
bars, she hid the rest behind her bookcase.

Throughout the day Harriet checked on her candy.

She counted it.

Then she hid it in a new place every time.

Pretty soon Harriet was running out of places to hide it.

"There's only one thing to do," said Harriet.
"I'll have to eat it all up."

So she started to eat. First chocolate bars with peanuts.

Then licorice whips. Then peanut-butter cups.

Then red, blue, green, and orange gumdrops.

"Burp," she said when she got to the saltwater taffy. "I don't feel so good."

"Maybe it's time to share."

"Wouldn't you like a sugar doughnut, Walt?"

"How about some caramel apples?"

"I'm so proud of you, Harriet," said Mother.
"Sharing is a sign of a grown-up dog."

"Oh," said Harriet, "I was going to share all the time."

"That's good, Harriet," said Mother. "Now go wash up for dinner."